CHAPTERS

CHAPTER ONE
THE FORT

Ricky Ricotta and his Mighty Robot sat on the front steps of their house. They were bored.

"We are going shopping," said Ricky's mother. "I don't want you boys making a mess while we are gone!"

"A *mess?*" said Ricky. "When have we ever made a mess?"

"Every time you jump in a mud puddle, you make a big mess," said Ricky's mother.

"Oh, yeah," said Ricky.

"And every time you climb a tree, you make a big mess!" said Ricky's mother.

"Oh, yeah," said Ricky.

"And every time you chew
bubble gum, you make a big mess!"
said Ricky's mother.
"Oh, yeah," said Ricky.

"I know," said Ricky's father. "Why don't you boys build a fort?"

"A *fort?*" said Ricky.

"Yes," said Ricky's father. "You can use tree branches, or cardboard boxes, or even old pieces of metal and wood to make a fort!"

"That sounds like fun," said Ricky.

"Great!" said Ricky's father. "Just remember, you must clean up after yourselves when you are done playing."
"We will," said Ricky.

"Good-bye," said Ricky's mother.
"And remember: NO MESSES!"
"Don't worry," said Ricky.

Ricky and his Mighty Robot walked around town looking for things they could use to make their fort.

Ricky found a stick.

Ricky's Mighty Robot found a piece of string.

Then Ricky and his Mighty Robot
found something even better.

At the edge of town, the mayor
and the city planner were looking
up at a rickety, old building.

"We must tear this old building down," said Mayor Munster.

"It will be a big job," said the city planner. "It will take lots of time and cost lots of money."

Ricky got an idea.

"Mr. Mayor," said Ricky, "my Mighty Robot will tear this building down for free if you let us keep all the pieces."

"Really?" said Mayor Munster. "It's a deal!"

So Ricky's Mighty Robot began
taking the building apart, piece by
piece. He stacked all the pieces in
a nice, neat pile.

"This is perfect!" said Ricky.
"Now we have everything we need
for our fort!"

CHAPTER TWO

THE MESS

Ricky and his Mighty Robot walked home with the gigantic stack of pieces for their fort. Ricky's parents were still out shopping, so his Mighty Robot threw all the pieces down in the backyard.

BOOM!

"What is going on over there?" cried Farmer Feta, the grumpy old mouse who lived next door.

"We are building a fort," said Ricky.

"Well, keep it quiet," said Farmer Feta. "You kids are much too noisy!"

"We will try," said Ricky.

Ricky and his Mighty Robot started building their fort. The Mighty Robot took some steel columns and pounded them into the ground.

BAM! BAM! BAM!

"Hey!" shouted Farmer Feta. "I thought I told you kids to keep quiet!"

"Sorry," said Ricky.

Next, the Mighty Robot used his laser eyes to weld metal girders to the steel columns.

ZZZZZ! ZZZZZZ! ZZZZZZZ!

"THAT'S *STILL* TOO MUCH NOISE!" cried Farmer Feta.

"Oops," said Ricky.

Then Ricky's Mighty Robot pounded wooden floorboards onto the metal girders.

BANG! BANG! BANG! BANG! BANG!

"YOU'RE DRIVING ME CRAZY!" shouted Farmer Feta.

"We'll be quieter," said Ricky. But Ricky and his Mighty Robot just got noisier and noisier. And Farmer Feta got angrier and angrier.

CHAPTER THREE
GUESTS

When Ricky's parents returned home, they saw the gigantic, towering fort that Ricky and his Robot had made.

Ricky's mother was not happy. "You boys are in BIG TROUBLE!" she said.

"It was Dad's idea!" said Ricky.

Ricky's dad was in big trouble, too.

"We are having guests over for dinner," said Ricky's mother. "I want that mess cleaned up right now!"

"But Dad said we didn't have to clean it up until *AFTER* we were done playing," Ricky said.

Ricky's dad was in even bigger trouble.

Ricky and his Mighty Robot played in their giant fort until their guests arrived.

When Uncle Freddie and Auntie Ethel pulled into the driveway, Lucy and her Jurassic Jackrabbits jumped out of the truck and bounded into the backyard.

"Wow!" said Lucy. "I love your new castle."

"It's not a castle," said Ricky. "It's a FORT!"

"That's silly," said Lucy as she climbed up the ladder. "Who ever heard of a princess living in a *fort?* Come on up, Fudgie! Climb aboard, Cupcake! Welcome to our new castle, Waffles!"

Lucy and her giant pets made themselves right at home.

. . . and Fudgie jumped up and down on the trampoline.

"What this place needs is some curtains," said Lucy. "And let's paint everything *PINK*!"

"But —" said Ricky.

Cupcake rode on the roller coaster,
Waffles swung on the swing . . .

"Oh, I just love the castle you built for us," said Lucy. "It's going to be SO PRETTY!"

"But —" said Ricky.

"You're the best cousin ever," said Lucy.

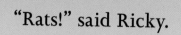

"Rats!" said Ricky.

CHAPTER FOUR
NIMROD NIGHTCRAWLER

Meanwhile, 267,556,222,000 miles away on the planet Neptune, a very naughty Nightcrawler was planning something nasty.

You see, Neptune had once been a very pleasant planet. But the greedy Nightcrawlers of Neptune started digging and digging for fossil fuels.

This produced so much methane gas that it blocked out the sun. Soon, the planet became cold, windy, and clouded over with thick, blue, poisonous vapor.

The Nightcrawlers had to move down into underground tunnels, where it was always cold and dark and creepy.

Neptune's greatest scientist, Nimrod Nightcrawler, had been studying the Earth for a very long time. He knew it was the nicest planet in our solar system, and he and his Nightcrawler army wanted it for themselves.

EARTH

But Nimrod had seen how villains from Mercury, Venus, Mars, Jupiter, Saturn, and Uranus were all defeated by Ricky Ricotta and his Mighty Robot.

Nimrod knew he must come up with a different plan of attack. Something sneaky . . . something slimy . . . something *wormy*!

Suddenly, Nimrod Nightcrawler got a very nasty idea.

He loaded a tiny rocket ship
with an inflatable wormhole,
and blasted it off.

The rocket ship flew through
the solar system, straight toward
the Earth.

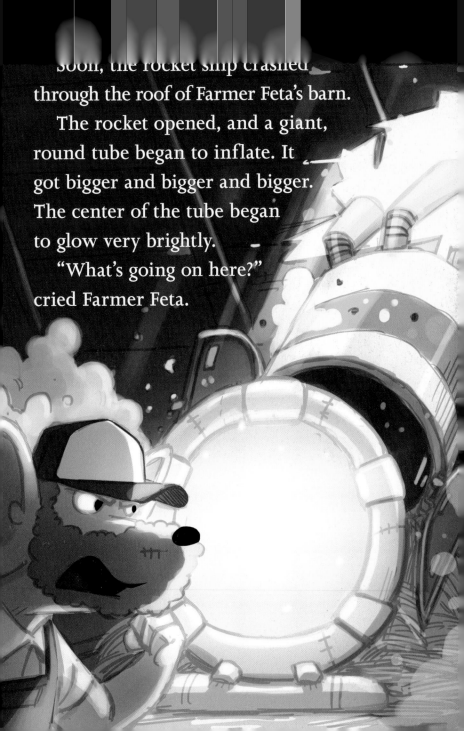

Soon, the rocket ship crashed
through the roof of Farmer Feta's barn.

The rocket opened, and a giant,
round tube began to inflate. It
got bigger and bigger and bigger.
The center of the tube began
to glow very brightly.

"What's going on here?"
cried Farmer Feta.

Back on Neptune, Nimrod Nightcrawler was staring at a giant, inflatable tube, too. "Here goes nothing," said Nimrod, and he poked his head into the glowing center of the tube.

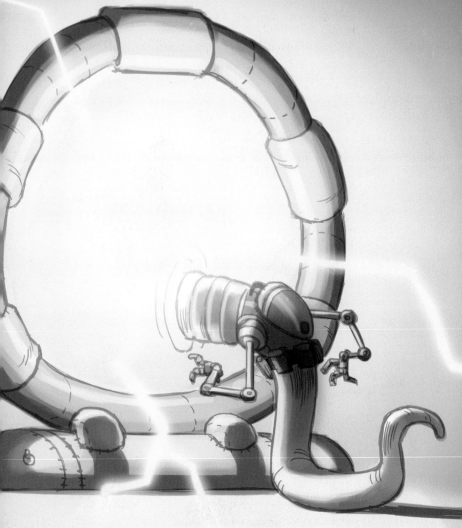

At that very moment, Nimrod's head poked OUT of the hole in Farmer Feta's barn.

"Greetings, Farmer Feta," said Nimrod. "I have come to Earth through this wormhole to help you with your problem."

"What problem?" asked the frightened farmer.

"Why, those noisy kids next door," said Nimrod.

"Oh, yeah," said Farmer Feta, as his mouth stretched into a sneer. "I can't stand those kids!"

"Well," said Nimrod, "if you let me dig a tunnel under your land, I can put a stop to those noisy pests once and for all!"

"Great!" said the farmer. "Dig away!"

"Let's go, boys!" said Nimrod.

Suddenly, five enormously naughty Nightcrawlers slithered out of the wormhole. They were dressed from head to tail in heavily armored Wiggle Worm Robo-Suits. A squishy, mechanical sound echoed through the barn as they pointed their robotic drill heads downward.

Soon, they began digging deep holes under the barn.

"Wait," said Farmer Feta. "You're not going to *hurt* those kids, are you?"

"Of course not," said Nimrod. "We're going to *DESTROY THEM!* HAW! HAW! HAW!"

CHAPTER FIVE
THE PIT

The Naughty Nightcrawlers from Neptune dug and dug and dug. Quickly, they made their way to the area underneath Ricky's fort.

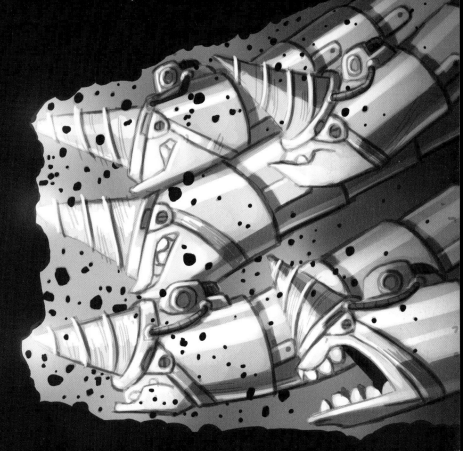

Up, up, up they tunneled,
until the earth below the fort was
hollow and unstable. Ricky's fort
began to creak and groan.

"What's wrong with my castle,
Ricky?" asked Lucy while the family
was eating dinner. "Why is it making
that noise?"

"I don't know," said Ricky.

Ricky's Mighty Robot walked over
to the fort. He checked the steel columns
as the fort swayed from side to side.
Then he kicked the ground gently
with his giant foot.

Suddenly, the earth below the Mighty
Robot's feet crumbled, and he fell into
a deep, dark pit.

"*Robot!*" cried Ricky. "Are you OK?"

Finally, Ricky's fort began to
rumble and bend.

"It's going to fall!" cried Ricky's
dad. "*RUN!*"

All at once, the heavy steel fort collapsed and came crashing down into the deep, dark pit.

Ricky's Mighty Robot was buried alive beneath the thick metal beams. He tried and tried, but he could not even move one inch. The Mighty Robot was trapped.

Ricky and his family tried to help the Mighty Robot, but they could not budge the metal girders.

CHAPTER SIX
THROUGH THE WORMHOLE

Back on Neptune, Ricky tumbled out of the wormhole and landed on the ground with a thud.

Lucy came through, too, followed by her three Jurassic Jackrabbits.

"Where are we?" asked Lucy.

"We must be on Neptune," said Ricky.

"How can you tell?" asked Lucy.

Ricky pointed up to the skylight.

"Thirteen moons," he said.
"Oh," said Lucy.

Quietly, the five friends tiptoed through the dark, cavernous tunnels.

First, they passed a heavily guarded supply room with lots of empty Wiggle Worm Robo-Suits.

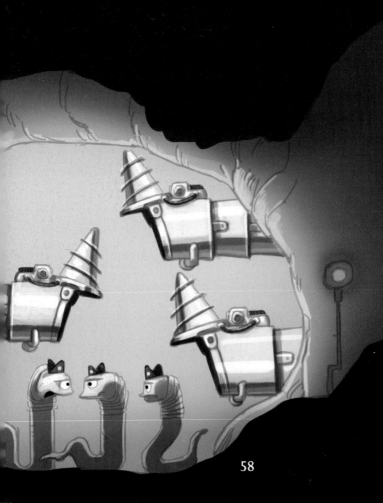

Waffles flew to get help. Right away
he noticed a bright light coming from
Farmer Feta's barn.

Ricky and Lucy decided to investigate.

"I've made a terrible, *terrible* mistake," said Farmer Feta, and he told everyone what he had done.

"Oh, well," said Ricky, "I guess there's only one thing to do!" He ran toward the glowing wormhole, jumped through the center, and disappeared.

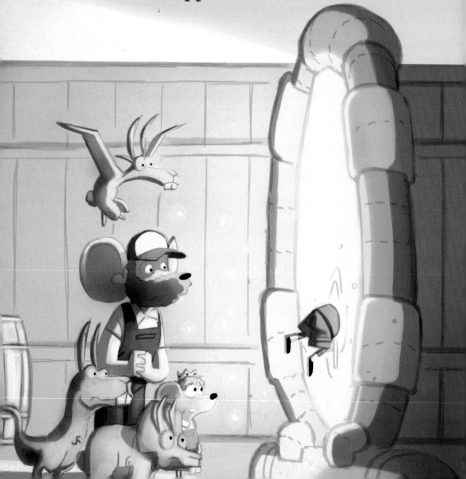

Next, they came to the TV room,
where several slimy Nightcrawlers
were huddled together in front
of the glowing video screens.

Fudgie and Cupcake got frightened.

They stepped backward . . .

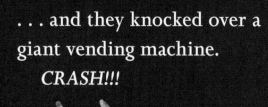

. . . and they knocked over a
giant vending machine.
CRASH!!!

The Nightcrawlers jumped when they heard the noise. They turned their slimy heads and saw our heroes.

"Destroy the intruders!" shouted the slimiest Nightcrawler of the bunch, and the chase began!

BOOM!

CHAPTER SEVEN
TRAPPED

Soon Ricky, Lucy, Fudgie, Cupcake, and Waffles were wrapped up tightly in a tangled, wormy pile of slithering Nightcrawlers.

"Gotta—fight—back!" cried Lucy.

"But *how?*" asked Ricky. "I can't even tell which ends are the heads and which ends are the tails!"

"Let's just tickle them in the middle and see which end laughs," said Lucy.

"Hey, good idea," said Ricky.

So Ricky and Lucy began to tickle their captors. The Naughty Nightcrawlers started to giggle and squirm.

Ricky and Lucy tickled more. The Naughty Nightcrawlers started to wiggle and laugh.

Finally, Ricky and Lucy tickled with all their might. The Naughty Nightcrawlers lost it. They let go of our heroes and rolled around on the ground, shrieking with laughter.

Fudgie, Cupcake, and Waffles started tickling the Nightcrawlers, too, and things just got sillier and sillier!

"Isn't this fun?" said Ricky. But nobody answered him. "Hey," he said. "Where is Lucy?"

Suddenly, a squishy, mechanical sound got louder and louder.

CRASH!

"Out of my way, ya dumb worms!" cried Ricky's crazy cousin as she sped by on a giant Wiggle Worm Robo-Suit. "Princess Lucy is *COMIN' THROUGH!*"

"Wait for us!" cried Ricky. He jumped up and ran after her. The Jurassic Jackrabbits followed Ricky. The Naughty Nightcrawlers followed them all.

Ricky, Fudgie, Waffles, and Cupcake followed Lucy down the dark tunnels until she disappeared through the center of the glowing wormhole.

Ricky and the Jurassic Jackrabbits
jumped through, too, and found
themselves back in Farmer Feta's
barn. But where was Lucy?

"Quick," cried Ricky. "The Nightcrawlers are right behind us! We've got to block off this wormhole so they can't get through!"

Ricky and the Jurassic Jackrabbits pushed a tractor toward the wormhole, but they were too late. The Naughty Nightcrawlers from Neptune started slithering through.

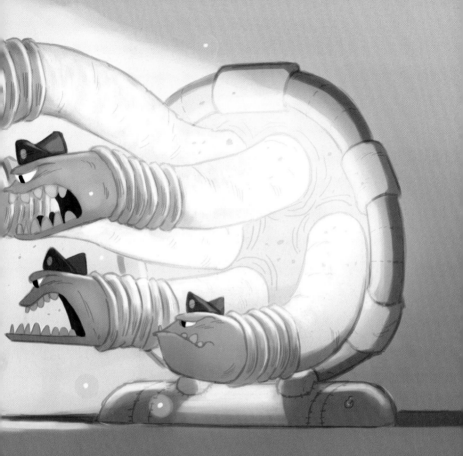

The slimy beasts wiggled through
the wormhole, until every inch
of the barn was squirming with
Nightcrawlers.

"Oh, NO!" cried Ricky. "We're
TRAPPED!"

CHAPTER EIGHT
THE RESCUE

Suddenly, the roof of the barn opened up. Ricky looked up and saw his old friend.

"Mighty Robot!" cried Ricky.
"You're BACK!"

"Yep," said Lucy. "I dug him up!"

When the Naughty Nightcrawlers from Neptune saw Ricky Ricotta's Mighty Robot, they screamed in horror. Quickly, they wiggled back into the wormhole, squirming for their lives!

"Gee, that was easy," said Lucy.

"Yes," said Ricky, "but the city is still under attack by those Robo-Worms!"

"Well, let's go get 'em!" cried Lucy.

THERE WILL
BE TROUBLE
INDEED...

...FOR YOU!!!

CHAPTER NINE
THE BIG BATTLE
(IN FLIP-O-RAMA™)

-RAMA
HERE'S HOW IT WORKS!

STEP 1

Place your *left* hand inside the dotted lines marked "LEFT HAND HERE." Hold the book open *flat*.

STEP 2

Grasp the *right-hand* page with your right thumb and index finger (inside the dotted lines marked "RIGHT THUMB HERE").

STEP 3

Now *quickly* flip the right-hand page back and forth until the picture appears to be *animated*.

(For extra fun, try adding your own sound-effects!)

FLIP-O-RAMA 1

(pages 91 and 93)

Remember, flip *only* page 91.
While you are flipping, be sure you
can see the picture on page 91
and the one on page 93.
If you flip quickly, the two
pictures will start to look like
<u>one</u> *animated* picture.

Don't forget to add
your own sound-effects!

LEFT HAND HERE

THE NIGHTCRAWLER ATTACKED.

RIGHT
THUMB
HERE

92

THE NIGHTCRAWLER
ATTACKED.

FLIP-O-RAMA 2

(pages 95 and 97)

Remember, flip *only* page 95.
While you are flipping, be sure you
can see the picture on page 95
and the one on page 97.
If you flip quickly, the two
pictures will start to look like
<u>one</u> *animated* picture.

Don't forget to add
your own sound-effects!

LEFT HAND HERE

THE MIGHTY ROBOT
FOUGHT BACK.

RIGHT
THUMB
HERE

RIGHT
INDEX
FINGER
HERE

96

THE MIGHTY ROBOT
FOUGHT BACK.

FLIP-O-RAMA 3

(pages 99 and 101)

Remember, flip *only* page 99.
While you are flipping, be sure you
can see the picture on page 99
and the one on page 101.
If you flip quickly, the two
pictures will start to look like
<u>one</u> *animated* picture.

Don't forget to add
your own sound-effects!

LEFT HAND HERE

THE NIGHTCRAWLER BATTLED HARD.

RIGHT
THUMB
HERE

THE NIGHTCRAWLER BATTLED HARD.

FLIP-O-RAMA 4

(pages 103 and 105)

Remember, flip *only* page 103.
While you are flipping, be sure you
can see the picture on page 103
and the one on page 105.
If you flip quickly, the two
pictures will start to look like
<u>one</u> *animated* picture.

Don't forget to add
your own sound-effects!

LEFT HAND HERE

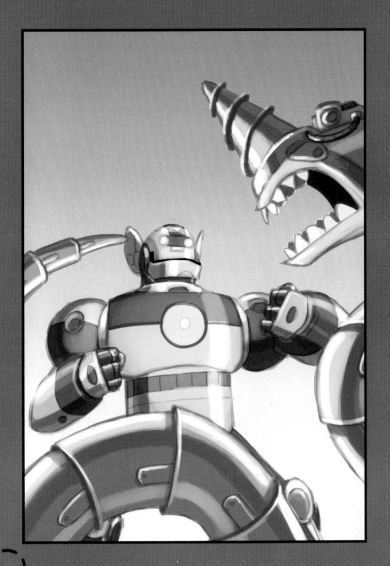

RICKY'S ROBOT
BATTLED HARDER.

RIGHT
THUMB
HERE

104

RICKY'S ROBOT
BATTLED HARDER.

FLIP-O-RAMA 5

(pages 107 and 109)

Remember, flip *only* page 107.
While you are flipping, be sure you
can see the picture on page 107
and the one on page 109.
If you flip quickly, the two
pictures will start to look like
<u>one</u> *animated* picture.

Don't forget to add
your own sound-effects!

LEFT HAND HERE

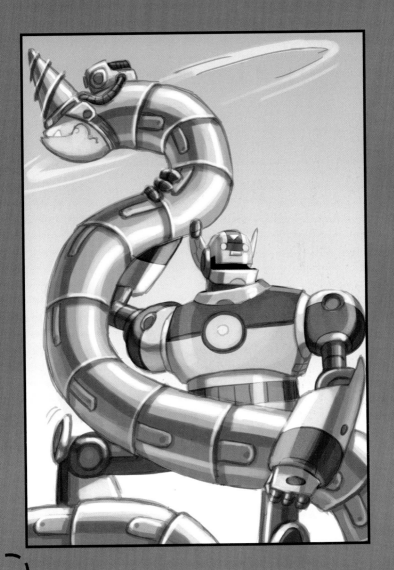

RICKY'S ROBOT
WON THE WAR.

RIGHT
THUMB
HERE

RIGHT
INDEX
FINGER
HERE

108

**RICKY'S ROBOT
WON THE WAR.**

CHAPTER TEN
A SQUIRMY SOLUTION

The Naughty Nightcrawlers from Neptune were defeated. They squirmed back to Farmer Feta's barn and escaped to Neptune through the wormhole.

"Come back here, you slithering idiots!" cried Nimrod.

Ricky Ricotta's
Mighty Robot picked
up Nimrod . . .

. . . and put him right where he belonged!

"Rats!" said Nimrod.

Soon, our heroes were home.

"What's for dessert?" asked Lucy.

"There will be NO DESSERT,"
said Ricky's mother, "until you
children clean up this mess!"

"Aw, man!" said Lucy.

"Hey, I have an idea," said Ricky.

He and Lucy and the Jurassic Jackrabbits went to Farmer Feta's barn and got the inflatable wormhole. They carried it to Ricky's house and set it down in the backyard.

Then they all started to clean.
Ricky's Mighty Robot picked up all
the giant pieces of junk and dropped
them into the wormhole. Ricky and
Lucy and her pets picked up the small
scraps and dropped them in, too.

All of the junk disappeared
from Ricky's backyard . . .

. . . and reappeared on Neptune.
CRASH!!!! BANG!!!! BOOM!!!!
THUD!!!! SMASH!!!!

The Nightcrawlers' computers were destroyed. Their technology was crushed. And the inflatable wormhole powered down forever.

"All done," said Ricky.

"What about that deep hole in the ground?" asked Ricky's mother.

"I know what to do," said Lucy.

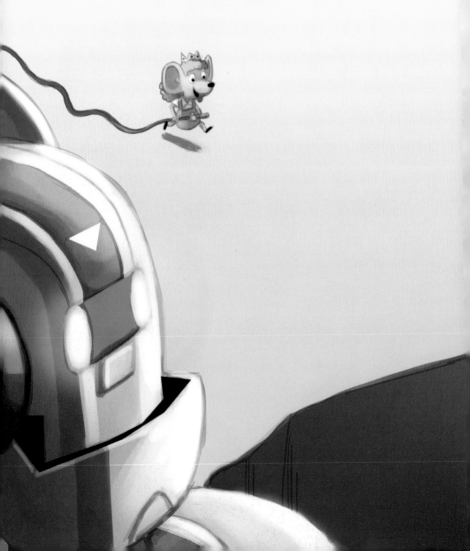

She took a garden hose from
the side of the house . . .

. . . and filled the hole up with water. "Now you have a pond!" said Lucy.

"Wow!" said Ricky's parents. "We've always wanted a pond!"

"Thank you," said Ricky's father, "for saving the world again!"

"And thank you for saving each other!" said Auntie Ethel.

"And thank you for working together," said Uncle Freddie.

"And thank you for cleaning up the mess!" said Ricky's mother.

"No problem," said Ricky . . .

. . . "that's what friends are for!"

READY FOR

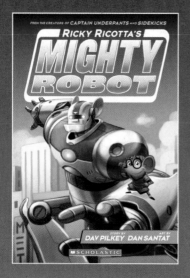

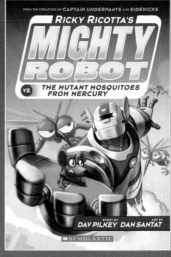

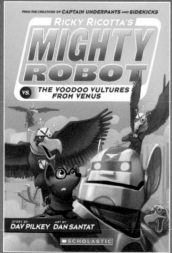

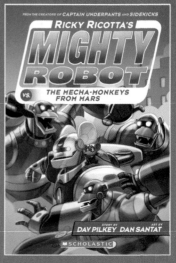

MORE RICKY?

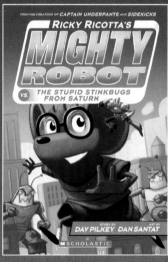

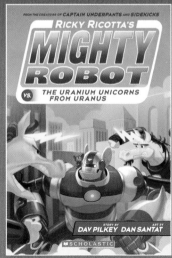

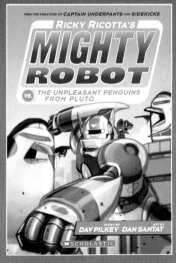

DAV PILKEY

has written and illustrated more than fifty books for children, including *The Paperboy*, a Caldecott Honor book; *Dog Breath: The Horrible Trouble with Hally Tosis*, winner of the California Young Reader Medal; and the IRA Children's Choice Dumb Bunnies series. He is also the creator of the *New York Times* best-selling Captain Underpants books. Dav lives in the Pacific Northwest with his wife. Find him online at www.pilkey.com.

DAN SANTAT

is the writer and illustrator of the *New York Times* bestselling picture book *The Adventures of Beekle: The Unimaginary Friend*, which was awarded the Caldecott Medal. He is also the creator of the graphic novel *Sidekicks* and has illustrated many acclaimed picture books, including *Because I'm Your Dad* by Ahmet Zappa and *Crankenstein* by Samantha Berger. Dan also created the Disney animated hit *The Replacements*. He lives in Southern California with his family. Find him online at www.dantat.com.